A Wacky, Rocky World

A Wacky, Rocky World

JUST A TEENY LITTLE VOICE

sheila atienza

Privilege Digital Media

A Wacky, Rocky World: Just a Teeny Little Voice
Copyright © 2021 by Sheila Atienza

Published by
Privilege Digital Media
Richmond, British Columbia
Canada

This book features a story, poems, words, and expressions, that describe
and depict a teenager's life using fictional characters. Any similarities to
any person or persons, places, and events are purely coincidental.

Paperback ISBN-13:
978-1-990408-05-2

E-book ISBN:
978-1-990408-06-9

Subjects:
YOUNG ADULT FICTION / Coming of Age
YOUNG ADULT FICTION / Poetry
YOUNG ADULT FICTION / Romance / Multicultural & Interracial

Thema Subjects:
Children's / Teenage personal and social topics: Friends and friendships
Children's / Teenage fiction: Relationship stories – Romance, love or
friendship
Bullying and harassment
Social groups and identities
Ethnic groups and multicultural studies
Children's / Teenage personal and social topics: Racism

CONTENTS

about this book

What happens when a biracial teenage boy starts to question what is going on in his world?

Life can be wonderful, right? But why does everything seem to be somewhat wacky and out-of-place?

This book "A Wacky, Rocky World: Just a Teeny Little Voice" features poems, expressions, and a story, as shared through the point of view of an *Asian-Canadian* fourteen-year-old boy named Rocky.

In honour of the spirit of multiculturalism and a fight against racism and bullying, this work came into existence. This book, which is suitable for all ages, aims to support such ideals.

words from the author

everyone is
a blessing
if you think about it

one can have a heart
that is
pure and innocent

what it takes
to keep growing
and be in tuned
with your well-being
is to have
an open mind
and to give
your sincere intent

-sincerely, the author

some excerpts

"no matter how i express it
through my words, still
to me, i feel
as though i am always
in some kind of a maze"
-maze

"we call on the moon
to witness our world
to bring out an even lighter mood
to feel the vibe from the outside
as it slowly kisses a slight dark night
to bring rhythm
and warmth"
- *first music and company*

"for a bit
i thought a life
of a teenager like
mine is nothing but
awkward, if not
simply redundant"
-*a little proud, a little good*

"true enough
i know where i should stand
the problem is with other people
they do not know where they stand"
-resemblance

"you know they say
i am in a stage
of this so-called life
when all i do
would seem to
end up
in an
embarrassment"
-a little proud, a little good

"everywhere
there is imbalance
who says life is fair
the very question i can't help but ask"
-imbalance and triggers

dedication

to the one
who looks forward
to a brighter path
despite the odds
cheers!

1

who gets it

a dull, even boring
voice is all i have got
but i keep it
within me

for why would not i
nobody does get me
nobody does seem
to be willing
to hear me out

only my heart could feel it
only my mind could comprehend
only my body can conceal
who gets it
but me
and i
alone

* * *

2

wasted, busted

sometimes, there, they are
in every corner
my *best friends*
as they claim
to be

oops
cross out the word *best*
in *best* friends
i will tell you why later
or how this
story goes
my mind is
shaken
even harder

here
let me start
again

as i told you
awhile ago

sometimes, there, they are
in every corner
my *(x) friends*
as they claim
to be

just like me
they also have many questions
i wonder
if they are
even thinking of their direction

but, they probably do not seem
to be
on the same page as
i am --

though, i wish
they could be
really be there
for me

they have their share of burdens
from their home
and even
from the people
they wish
they could relate
or they could be with—

but then
they could end up
busted

all attempts
one could try
from day one to the last
and all of which could end up
wasted

* * *

3

who is kidding

even asking mom and dad
seem to be
a big no-no
to no end

it is, as they say
closer to impossibility

all you could perhaps
hear--
is a resounding
voice
not a music
to your ears

"my darling
you must be kidding
very soon, you will forget it
you will not even
care about it."

but hey
if you hear it that way
everyday
it becomes more of
a resounding
noise
hardly you can
turn it off
and you would want
to rebut
and say
enough, enough

who is kidding
as i am not
who is not being
serious here
i would say i am not

you see
i am serious as ever
so why not give me
a little bit of control
can i not handle
things
my way
i mean, to a certain
extent

just trust me
is that too much
of my asking
and just to say it again
i am serious, i am not
kidding

* * *

4

who sees us

why can't they see us
the way we see ourselves

why can't they get us
the way they should, and yet

they expect us
to shut

why does it seem so hard
for us to ask

a simple request
they could not grant

have they not been
to the same place
as we are today

what do they fear
what do they
think about

are we not
vulnerable
are we not able
to catch
the ball

don' they
care
how we feel
and--

how would we react
when they say --

oh no, you cannot
do that
my dear
oh please, do not

* * *

5

maze

no matter how i put it in
my thoughts, still
to me, everything
looks like
a puzzle

there has
to be a way
to solve it

no matter how i express it
through my words, still
to me, i feel
as though i am always
in some kind of a maze

there has
to be a way
to get out of it

"i don't understand it," such
a common phrase
i always, always
say to myself
in many, many days

from the time i leave my class
and even
when i reach home
hoping i could relax

* * *

6

such a lame name

my name is *Rocky*
i shall not divulge my last name

not that i am forbidden
by my parents

why would they forbid me
for using their last name

i am theirs
even though i am somewhat
different

my sister, *Elena (as my parents call her)*
wants me to call her *El*
but she's okay with her real
name, or even to call her *Elaine*

unlike me
she would often
display
our last name
wherever
she could, she would put it
along with her
first name
El or *Elaine*

maybe their teachers
call them
by their last name
ahead of their first name

as for me
i like simple things
nothing fancy, nothing
grand

call me like i am
plain vanilla, boring, lame
as a child, as a playmate
as a student
i just would like others
to call me that way

yes, i am *Rocky*
call me by that name

* * *

7

blessing or curse

i'm not sure if one
could
look at my situation
as a blessing

being a kid of parents
who are
noteworthy
for their achievements
(that's what i would like to think)

my dad
defends
families and even
would-be singles

i mean those who are in the process
of trying to get separated from
their other half -
a husband or a wife
they would be single
eventually
and then
one or two could try again
to mingle
with a new other-half

my mom
does
a noble job
as a school nurse
my dad, of course
admires her the most

but on some weekends
she would go to
a community school
where she volunteers
as an *ESL* teacher
to do such a thing, she recalls
it is one of her goals

she guides many kids
who recently immigrated
to our neighbourhood
so that they could
learn to speak
English
as their second language
and also they could learn
how to relate and
to communicate and
to be understood well

about my sister *El*
not sure what
she wants to be
or what course or program
she would take up
when she graduates from
grade twelve

both my mom and dad
had asked her
many times
to give her answer
she was ever
reluctant

i asked her
one time
she said, it was hard
for her
to decide

for one
dad tells her
she can be a lawyer

but mom would tell her
it's okay if she wants
to be a nurse
or a teacher

hello, did you get what i mean
if you didn't
it's okay

i didn't get it either
the first time
but then—
i just have to hear her out

you know
she's my sibling
and my one and only

i wonder
if that's too bad
should i be sad
that—
i don't have a brother

maybe if i have one
he would be someone
cool and awesome
who could get me and
my thoughts, my wishes
and one can bet as
i will be fine

but, well
my sister *El*
has
a mind
of her own
i like her just the same

she may not know what
she wants
after all, she's only
seventeen

should she care about it
not sure, at this point

i even wonder the same
she tells me, she could decide later on

i heard her many times
she was telling me
our parents
could not just let her be

having a mom and a dad
who, together, had led a life
as meaningful as
they could
they have set
high standards

who could question
such an experience
in which others
consider
a blessing

but my sister was
on
the opposite fence

all she kept saying or asking
"*Was this a curse?*"

* * *

8

a silent 'me' story

okay, this is my story
i do not forget that

but mine
was such
a very unexciting one

nobody would want
to hear it
no one wants how i sound

someone
would rather dance
even the girl at school
whom
i truly want

her name
is *Jen*
she is white and
i am *Asian*

not sure if that is cool
i am not even
confident
to approach her at school

you know, i am used to
staying
in one
corner of our classroom
and remain silent
as much as i can

nobody
wants to know my story
i am *Rocky*
i am not their kind

* * *

9

attention-seeker

other students are so proud
they stay in a group
so they could be loud
as much as they wanted
and as much as they could

not sure if that is on
purpose
i did not hear much of their
essays and prose

they like to laugh and
brag
without courteousness
about something that
is not
funny nor
worthy
of one's gaze or
attention

i could see other
students
just playing along

some, perhaps get them
but most of us
do not

should i care
somehow, probably
i thought, i should
what do i do, what do i say

i see my fave girl *Jen*
was quite bothered
by this guy we call *Mon*

he wants to win
Jen's attention

* * *

10

not white, not brown

i remember
my first day at
middle school

i hardly
can speak out

not that i do not want
to talk
or anything like
that

it was just
that i was
reluctant

i could see
other students
are more aggressive
and they tend to be
very good at it
while a few students
tend to be
quite submissive

and i wonder
how others
would look at me
how would they speak—
to me

i am okay
with language
i speak *English* well
i was born here after all
like my sister, *El*

it was just that
my skin colour was
kind of different

when most students
are predominantly white
how do they look at
someone
whose colour is brown

then one student
approached me
he is not white
he is not brown like
me
but black

he said
i could call him *Robbie*
and then i said
i am *Rocky*

* * *

11

first acquaintance

funny how it came about
our names
Rocky and Robbie sound
very much alike
and even rhyme
to the max

we could even
rap to a beat
as we bike
on our way out

and—
i could no longer
count
how many days went by
at school, we were having fun
we were laughing
we were enjoying
we were biking
day in and
day out until a new day sets in

my very first
acquaintance is
a genuine, loyal one

we could
both look forward
to many, many years

we could be buddies
we could grow
together through
these years
at school

and even
through our world
outside
school

i thought
i've seen
a real gem, in him
an only true pal i've ever found

since then
Robbie
and i would share fun

i believe in *Robbie*
on him, i could count

* * *

12

what buddy could be to me

need i say
how much fun
would have i missed
on school days
without my buddy, *Robbie*

you bet
a day could be a misery for
a boy who is different
from their kind

a boy who would not
want anything but a simple
dull, quiet
school life

but with buddy, *Robbie*, i could
explore
and i could be
comfortable

my buddy, *Robbie*
my one and only friend
he is the one
who could fit the description
of a best friend

did i not mention earlier
i do not see any other
friend
whom i could refer
to as a true best friend
it's only *Robbie*
who can
somehow get me

it may not exactly be
the way i would navigate my boring world
and many other
things in my life

but at least
he knows i could go from
point one to eight
and back to one again

no other questions
that could ruin my day
and—
he is
being real
and that i could tell

* * *

13

assertive move

unlike me
Robbie is
way more assertive

he knows his
weakness
and he knows
what he can achieve

one day he noticed while
we were inside
the classroom
my eyes
were centered
on *Jen*, a girl
of my wishes

Robbie asked me
if i was interested
to befriend
Jen

i was stunned
with what i have heard
how could i ever get started
i was not sure about
the whole thing, you bet

she might just ignore me
who is *Rocky*, to her
anyway, i am no one
and i am not popular

but before i
could respond to him
i already bumped into *Jen*

not sure what happened
was there some kind
of a miracle or trick
that *Robbie* did—

Jen was smiling and
she's very gentle
she is
very kind
to me, she is
very pretty, i was captured, attracted
by her sweet smiles and her dimples
she is
very warm, very simple

must i be lucky that day
i got a little closer
to the girl
i truly like in school
Jen is very cool

of course
i would be grateful
to *Robbie*
my friend
for being the bridge
between me
and Jen

* * *

14

art, artsy

i got along
well with my lady friend, *Jen*
we are both doing fine
we both like art

we both like that part
in which we expressed
how we appreciate
colours and shapes
and even sounds

in every piece of work
be it visual
music or
performing arts

there
probably is no limit
even to try
to go unconventional

we are open to explore
and we can be unique

or we could roar
like a lion
and be sharp or
bold
that could call
attention

or
we could opt to be timid
shy away
stay low-key
like my usual self

o, the wondrous world of art
where different colours
can be more
predominant

in here, we allow our
wings to soar

in here i exist
in here my world would persist

* * *

15

round and round

i have not been more inspired
than today

and even
on many more
days to come
i will continue to be more
than alert
and
motivated

just like art
i am intrigued
where this thing
could take and lead me
every waking day

and now, what else
could i think about

i do not seem to be
bothered
anymore
by the presence of various forces
that could only cause more worries
in my thoughts
like what i had experienced
before

all i could think
about
is to continue
to hear myself out

through music
through its fast beat
or sometimes
even through a not
so fast beat
i feel as though
i'm in cloud nine
that my world is finally mine

i could be myself
i could tell myself
my little achievements
are finally in line

my environment
appears as though
it goes round and round
then it could go static
but only for a bit

and then it goes back
again in circle
and —
it would keep moving
round and round

* * *

16

facing a risky world

in a week's time
i am
turning
fourteen

perhaps, that could be exciting
another year is happening
though i'm not
a big
believer of big
parties, and i tell
my mom and dad
i do not want
to hold any of that
sorts

but my parents
might insist
and what could i do
but beg and request
another please

please, please
do not hold parties
for i don't want to celebrate this
way
i just have a simple wish
to perform music with
a few people on my list

they say, being
at your fourteenth
you are facing
a very dangerous thing --
a world that you can
create for your own being

can this be exciting
it is for me to find out and
see what surprises might it bring

* * *

17

first music and company

on the eve of my
fourteenth natal day
two friends of mine
went out of their way
to spend hours
and celebrate
a late afternoon fun

we were at my place
on our two-storey house
at the basement
just me, *Robbie and Jen*

Robbie brought his bass
guitar
i play the acoustic
guitar

Jen renders
her —
singing voice
charming and sweet
as we
play along with
some
modern tunes, and
even
some familiar classics

our very first music
with meaningful lyrics
we utter
some words and phrases

then—
we hit
some melodies
that match with
our moods, our feelings

that late afternoon
oh so awesome
it was as though
we call on the moon
to witness our world
to bring out an even lighter mood
to feel the vibe from the outside
as it slowly kisses a slight dark night
to bring rhythm
and warmth
to embody our chosen cycle of time
we all wish to feel
to be united
as though we could be immortal
and we would never part
as this teeny little world we create
could be eternal

* * *

18

monotonous not

i think
everyone would agree with me
with--
how a typical life can be

you see
life is never static
though it
can be monotonous or erratic

sometimes
life can be dramatic
it probably is because
of the influences
we see around, then
we pause
a moment
and notice
how it touches our senses

like seeing my mom watching
a never-ending *TV* drama series
okay, that was kind of exaggerated
of course, i forgot
even a show of that kind
ends, just like reality in life

Robbie's reality
Jen's reality
my reality
we all face reality
and that soon, we will all say
goodbye
we will all send a kiss
to our school heydays

summer
will soon kick in
and--
each of our families
has a plan

it can be the usual
summer
or it can be something radical

not sure how the season
will unfold its direction
that is a question
from all of us and it has been going on

as for me
one thing is sure
i cannot be in control
of how i should spend
my summer

as dad and mom
can push their
agenda, maybe good for them
but not for me

darn, what a life i have
i'm fourteen, aren't i
what changes do i expect
this is my life
this is *Rocky's* life

and--
even my sister
could not do anything
but to keep it
the way we got used to
the way we were
seeing the same view
and if we could be lucky
we could see our life on the other end
not monotonous
not dramatic, but humorous
who knows what summer
could teach us
in the end
Rocky's life can
be outrageous
but, of course
i hope to have fun

let's see how this life of ours would go
as we anticipate
the summer's heat
still hoping for some miracle
with some drum beats
there is messaging we all know
and we could do
some video call

and --
perhaps, if heavens could smile on us
amid the remoteness
we could find some goodness in it
that may be good for all

if only we could find our way
to bring together
food and music
that would be wonderful

* * *

19

resemblance

with open arms, i welcome
summer in *Okanagan*
with dad and mom
and *El,* my sister
we were all
prepping up on our way
to the lake

i heard mom invited other
family members
my aunts, uncles, and cousins
i thought that was interesting
at least
i could get
to meet
some people of my origin

you see, my dad is white
he is very much *Canadian*
Oops
that was wrong
of course
now i remember he mentioned
part of his ancestry is from
Europe and
America
i think he is also a little bit *French*
my sister *El* has more of a resemblance
to my dad than my mom

and even
with skin colour
one would not think of *El*
my sister
to be of *Asian*
in origin

but my sister said that
such a perspective is only relevant
to some groups of people

and most of those who would think that
she is very white
would come from the people (of our same colour)

according to her
when she is with
a group of many white people
they all
seem to know that
she is not
of the same kind
she is not a hundred percent white
she must have come from
some other background

so, for my sister, *El*
she is somewhere
in the middle
as she describes herself

somehow, she said, i am better off
being more of
an *Asian* look
at least, i know where i stand
or where i belong, on that end

true enough
i know where i should stand
the problem is with other people
they do not know where they stand

* * *

20

ethnic and culture 101

i must say
it is getting a little exciting
perhaps
it is even more appropriate
to describe that day
to be such an
awakening experience

i met *Titas and Titos*
such names are the *Filipinos'*
way of addressing
your aunts and uncles

i met, as well
their children, who are of the same age as i
and *El*

too many of them, and one could see
they were all
candid
taking pictures, wearing a smile
sitting from one place to another

then comes food time
everyone brought their potluck
some have *adobo* and egg with rice
some have *lumpia* or spring roll
and just like the rest
most foods are best served with rice

my mom made her version
she calls her special *Pancit Bihon*
it is
a kind of *Filipino* noodle dish
with mixed veggies
and some meat in it

of course, there are some more
foods that i am not familiar
not sure
how they call these foods, and even
some desserts and mostly rice-based oh
but they seem
to enjoy whatever
might be the ingredients

then, i could hear
Titos and Titas talking about some
celebrities
and then some politicians

you know, life back there
in the *Philippines*
my mom was avid and was listening
though i could not care

i almost could not notice
the beautiful, breathtaking scenery
in the *Okanagan Valley*

when you are with awesome people
like with my mom's extended families
all that matters are the experiences and
laughter that everyone exhibited
at those very moments

anyhow, we still have time to explore
the *Okanagan* points of interests
we were in *Kelowna,* and
from many different angles,
we could see on the shore
many, many more
pine forests and trees

oh, the beauty of nature
it is truly captivating
i am in awe, and
in my mind, i could paint
a picture

* * *

21

a little proud, a little good

for a bit
i thought a life
of a teenager like
mine is nothing but
awkward, if not
simply redundant

you know they say
i am in a stage
of this so-called life
when all i do
would seem to
end up
in an
embarrassment

while
somehow that
might be true
but there could always
be some instances
when my days
could end up
not
totally blue

like seeing
and enjoying
my little winnings

yes, i could win
in some board games
and even
in some chess games
and of course, in
my favourite computer games

it would seem
in those occasions
i could say
i am a little proud
i feel a little good
Rocky is in the mood

* * *

22

refreshed yet stunned

what could i say
my last
summer experience was
somewhat unexpected
a little different

it was
surprisingly fun
my experience was
kind of awesome
and i felt fine

i must admit
i felt a little
refreshed
yes
i could smile
i could look forward
to another
feel good summer

but for now
i am even
more excited
to call on my friend
my sweet, sweet, *Jen*
i can't wait
to hear her story on
the other line

but when
i am about to dial
the number keys on my phone
i could hear a buzzing sound
it was *Robbie* on the other line
so i picked up
the call

in a flash
there he is and his stories
i can't wait to hear
i'm sure
he's got some fun news

i listened intently to *Robbie's* voice
it was not
something i expected
i was stunned

i could not
believe
from what
i heard

* * *

23

what, why, where, when

i got so many questions
the moment
i learned
the not so good news
Robbie is moving
to another school

i asked him
what happened
he said they have to
but i said, that wasn't cool

Robbie was a bit silent
on the other line
i could sense he was
trying to compose
his words
i respected that
for a bit
i was also quiet

to be honest
i did not know how to react
there, i know my friend
needs someone
perhaps, a helping hand

i could not help it
and asked
why all of a sudden
they would have to leave

then
Robbie continued to speak
and
he said
because
his older brother got into
an accident, he was
in a fight
it was bad
or so to say in trouble
it was terrible

i heard *Robbie* telling
about a gang
for which the police was looking
Robbie could not
speak much about it
his voice was cracking
he was shaking and
almost trembling

he said he will be in touch
he would let me know
where and when
are they relocating

* * *

24

a sad opening

on my first day
back
to school
Jen approached me
on our way
to our classroom

she said, "Hey, *Rocky*
what's up?"
Jen asked more questions

i just smiled at her
but she knows
something was wrong
i could not elaborate further

but *Jen* could sense
i was not in myself
as though my spirit
was detached from my whole body
as i remained quiet

i could see *Jen* looking at me
as though i am lifeless
as i am without energy

i look pale and almost queasy, crappy
as though i am sick, she has no idea
i am missing
my best friend *Robbie's* presence

i broke the news, nevertheless
Jen was
also shocked
just how i reacted the first time i heard it
from *Robbie* himself

Jen also wonders and has
too many questions
i told her what i know so far
but our class
was about to start

* * *

25

imbalance and triggers

everywhere
there is imbalance
who says life is fair
the very question i can't help but ask

i may not understand
such things that are happening
but we see things
we could feel, sometimes, even the nonsense

at school alone, you have
to be tough
blend in
if you want to survive

there are
bullies in every corner of the school building
where could you go
and how do you keep hiding

it would seem, wherever side you go
there will always
be triggers
some may feel weak
and others will take
advantage

outside the school
it's even scarier
as you may face
an unknown occurrence

sometimes, you will have
to fight for your life
be strong
do some kicks
believe
you will survive

* * *

26

getting out of whack

my mom
saw me in a not so good
mood
as i approached
the door of our
home

she noticed there
was weariness
in me, in how i look
she said i must be tired
on my first day back to school

could you hide
something from someone
perhaps, some could do that
with--
no problem
and will be just fine

the case was different
with me and my mom

she has her way of finding out
so what's the point of hiding
she would insist
in asking
even if
i would refuse to speak

just right now, she knows something was
bothering me to the max
i can't concentrate
and she couldn't help but ask
besides, i couldn't contain it to myself
as i am worried about my friend *Robbie*
and i am somewhat agitated
things are getting out of whack

my mom said that i should take
a deep breath
find a way to
channel my energy

take a walk
listen to some music as i
used to do or play
my guitar, if i can
watch some movies
or do some games

and then rest
another day, i shall witness
the brightness of day, i shall kiss
i will be able to smile once again

* * *

27

embracing

mom was right
she said what was happening was relatable

she has her share of experiences that
made her questioned herself
and she didn't know how to respond any better

many people
were intrigued about her
when she first moved in here
as a *Canadian* immigrant
being an *Asian* herself
it was hard
when many people
look way different than you are

but she managed well
she worked as a caregiver first
then she devoted some time
to learn about the culture, to dwell
and embrace new ways
from the way
people communicate
to how they see and appreciate
things, here and there

then she became a nurse
that has been one of her goals
and she was very content, of course

she said many people are good
you will find a few who could
block your way
but your optimism
could
keep you going

know in your heart
what you want
be nice and kind
that's the key to a life
that you are making for yourself
and for your future self

* * *

28

with creative flair

in our class
the next day, we were asked
to write something
or think of anything that appeals to us
as a subject

then, do it with creative flair
do it with free-verse
or whatever style

there is no rule
just keep our ideas flowing

Jen has just finished her reading
she looked my way and smiled

she whispered, "You can do it, *Rocky.*"
i smiled back at her
i smiled at our teacher
then, i looked at everybody
i feel nervy, but who cares
i am ready to utter
my first lines and phrases
and whatever emotions i could express

and so, here i go:

there is no escaping
your reality will keep on haunting
you, in this world
to take part
and fill your heart

no one will
do that part
but you
and you alone
you have got to trust yourself
life is good
if you treat yours that way
if you look at others the same way
that's a golden rule we set each day

you build a life as though you deal
with a composition of a song or music
you have words, make them your lyrics
you compose some hymns and melodies
you learn and laugh, with your life
as though you solve a puzzle
you look for many missing elements
then you combine some bits and pieces

my life can be wacky
but in my little world
i am simply *Rocky*

* * *

~ the end ~

about the author

Sheila Atienza is a Canadian book author, digital media artist, and marketing professional based in B.C., Canada. She is also an award-winning filmmaker, actress, and passionate content creator.

Sheila explores nonfiction, fiction, and poetry. Some of her published works/books are available in:

University of Toronto Thomas Fisher Library; McGill University; Dalhousie University DAL Killam Library; Brown University; Library and Archives nationales du Québec; Canada Mortgage Housing Corporation; Medicine Hat College; Loyalist College; and other libraries across Canada and the U.S.A.

Sheila's books are also available through bookstores and online retailers worldwide.

also by the author

Other Fiction and Poetry

Beauty in Love and Sorrows

Feed and Discern:
Some Words of Wisdom, Some Poems, Some Life Lessons

Tweets for Your Thoughts